Smart Dad

Written and illustrated by Amanda Graham

An easy-to-read SOLO
for beginning readers

SOLOS

Southwood Books Limited
3-5 Islington High Street
London N1 9LQ

First published in Australia by Omnibus Books 1997

This edition published in the UK under licence from
Omnibus Books by
Southwood Books Limited, 2002

Text and illustrations copyright © Amanda Graham 1997

Cover design by Lyn Mitchell

ISBN 1 903207 55 X

Printed in Hong Kong

A CIP catalogue record for this book is available
from the British Library

For my smart dad,
who made a wonderful boat

Chapter 1

Dad is smart.

He can do anything.

He made a big kennel for Spotty, a huge tree-house for Anna and me, and a giant letterbox for Mum.

Dad always says, "Big is best."

Dad had plans for something new.
One night he showed them to us.
"We'll make a boat," he said "
and sail to Spain in July."
"Cool," Anna and I shouted.

"Mmmm." Mum looked like she was thinking about the letterbox.

"We'll make the boat in our own back garden," said Dad. "You can all help."

Chapter 2

The timber came on a big truck.

My best friend Jerry came over to help.

Carefully we traced shapes onto sheets and planks of wood.

Dad cut them out with a saw, then we glued and clamped the shapes together.

There was a *lot* to do.

Chapter 3

After a few weeks there was a skeleton boat in our back garden.

"It's not quite right, Mr Green," said Jerry. "It looks upside-down!"

"That's the way you make a boat, Jerry." Dad sounded a bit grumpy. "When the hull is ready, everybody in the street can help us turn it over."

"It's very *big*," said Mum.

"It *needs* to be big to fit us all on board," said Dad.

"Big enough for Jerry to come too?" I asked. I crossed my fingers. "Not this time, Jack," said Mum.

Chapter 4

One night Mum gave us our life-jackets.

We played Lost at Sea in the bath.

Poor Spotty was sea-sick all over the bathroom floor.

I told Mum.

"Jerry never gets sea-sick. Perhaps
he could come instead of Spotty."

"Maybe next time," said Mum.

Chapter 5

July was getting closer. The boat
was still upside-down.

"Will it ever, ever be finished?"
I asked.

"Sooner or later," smiled Dad.
I wasn't so sure.

Chapter 6

The next afternoon everyone in the street was in our back garden.

"One, two, three ... *lift!*" Dad called out in a loud voice.

The hull of the boat rose into the
air like magic.

"Now, gently … gently …"
It began to roll over.

Before you could blink twice, the boat was the right way up.

Everyone clapped and cheered.
"Tea and buns for all of us!"
said Dad.

Chapter 7

July was *very* close.

There was still a deck to be made, the mast to be fitted and sails to be sewn.

Making a boat is heaps of work.

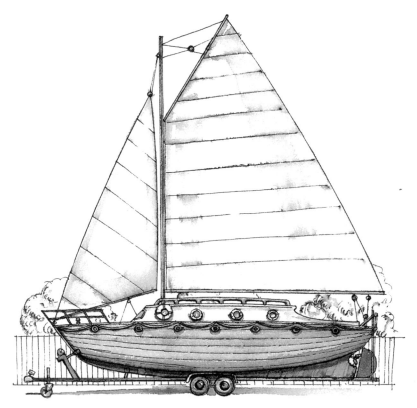

Chapter 8

Wow!

The last rope had been tied and the last plank painted.

Our boat was finished.

It was the biggest boat I had ever seen.

"Now," said Dad, "it's time to pack the car. Tomorrow we sail."

Yippeeee!!!

Chapter 9

The alarm went off very early next
morning. But it was easy to get up.
Much easier than for school.

"We're ready to go," yelled Dad.

Anna and I ran to open the front gates.

It was Mum's job to watch the boat from behind.

Spotty just jumped about and yapped a lot.

Dad turned into the driveway between our house and Mr Clark's brick garage.

Suddenly Mum started yelling,
"Stop! Stop!"

We heard a loud noise. Dad
slammed on the brakes.

Oh no! Had Spotty been squashed under the trailer?

I raced down the driveway.

Chapter 10

Spotty was fine, but Dad was not.

His face turned white when he saw what was wrong.

The boat was wide.

Far too wide.

It would never go down our narrow driveway.

The front had already scraped the house.

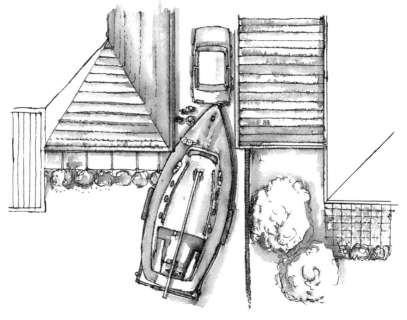

The boat was stuck in our back garden *forever*.

"I don't believe it," said Dad.
He shook his head slowly. Then he
went off to his shed to think.

Just great. We would never get to Spain.

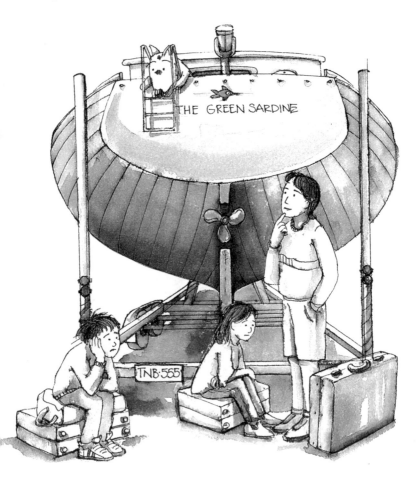

THE GREEN SARDINE

TNB·555

Chapter 11

It was dark outside when Mum knocked on our bedroom doors.

I couldn't tell if it was morning or night.

"Quickly, Anna! Quickly, Jack! Wake up! We're going on our holiday."

"Dad's worked out how to get the boat out," said Anna.

"Cool," I shouted.

I ran to the car, but this time there was no boat hooked behind.

What was going on?

"The camping gear is packed. Let's go," said Dad.

A camping holiday? Yuk! Who wants to go camping when you've got a boat in your back garden.

Chapter 12

Anna and I fell asleep in the car.

We didn't wake up until we arrived. It was still pitch black. I couldn't see a thing.

"What camping spot is this?" I asked.

"It's a big surprise. Wait until morning," said Mum as she laid out my sleeping-bag. "Now, off to sleep."

Chapter 13

Big surprise? It was a *huge* surprise.
When I poked my head out of the tent in the morning, I saw sand and blue water.

I saw palm trees and fish.

It was just like Spain. Except it wasn't Spain.

Chapter 14

We must have driven round in circles all night, because we were parked in our own back garden. It looked just like a desert island.

There were Mr Clark's rubber plants, Max-from-next-door's fish and the wading pool from Jerry's house.

And in the middle of it all was our boat.

"We couldn't take our boat to the beach," said Mum, "so we had to bring the beach to our boat."

"Cool!" said Anna and I together.

"All hands on deck," shouted Dad, "and let's set sail for the best boat holiday ever."

Chapter 15

It wasn't quite the holiday we had dreamed of. Our back garden was a long way from Spain.

But in some ways it was even better than being at sea.

Spotty didn't get sea-sick.

Mum didn't worry about us falling overboard.

And, best of all, Jerry could
come too.

Next year, Dad says, we'll make it to the real sea.

By then we will have saved enough money to pay for a crane to lift the boat out.

Or maybe my smart Dad has another plan ...

Amanda Graham

When I was six, my dad made a boat. Everybody helped, even Woofa the dog!

The best thing was when we launched it. How awful if you made a boat, but then you couldn't get it into the water! This gave me the idea for *Smart Dad*.

Looking at books about boats helped me to work out what kind of boat Smart Dad would have made. Remembering the way my dad made our boat helped me too.